Bad Boris
goes to school

For Mum and Dad Jenkin, with love

A RED FOX BOOK

Published by Arrow Books Limited
20 Vauxhall Bridge Road, London SW1V 2SA

An imprint of Random Century Group

London Melbourne Sydney Auckland Johannesburg
and agencies throughout the world

First published in Great Britain in hardback in 1989
by Hutchinson Children's Books
Red Fox Edition 1990

Text © Susie Jenkin-Pearce 1989

Printed and bound in Great Britain by
Scotprint, Musselburgh, Scotland

ISBN 0 09 964620 X

Bad Boris
goes to school

Susie Jenkin-Pearce

RED FOX

'Boris,' said Maisie one morning, 'you're old enough to go to school.'

'School!' gasped Boris. 'No I'm not. I hate school!'

'Nonsense,' said Maisie. 'You'll do painting and writing. You'll learn to read and play lots of games. You'll *love* it!'

'No I won't,' growled Boris.

'Wish I could go,' said the kitten.

But Boris just flattened his ears and refused to listen.

The next day, they all went out to buy Boris's school things.

They bought pencils,

a pack of felt-tip pens,

a painting
apron,

and a lunch box.

Boris didn't even say thank you. 'I hate school,' was all he said.

But all young elephants must go to school and soon it was Boris's first day.

The classroom was full of excited animals saying hello to their friends from last term, and there were some new animals looking a bit scared.

'This is Boris,' said Maisie to Mrs Prism, the teacher.

When the grown-ups had gone, Mrs Prism called the noisy animals together. 'Hush, now,' she said. 'You're as noisy as a class full of children.'

Boris found himself next to a small crocodile who couldn't stop crying. 'Don't cry,' he said. 'I'll look after you.'

The morning went very quickly. They did painting, then music and movement.

First they pretended to be fire-breathing dragons. Then Mrs Prism let them choose something for themselves.

'I'm a tree,' cried Boris, 'swaying in the breeze.'

At lunchtime, Boris and the crocodile shared their sandwiches. The crocodile ate one of Boris's buns. She was already feeling a lot happier.

In the afternoon they played with sand and...

water.

Mrs Prism seemed very pleased with Boris. His trunk was just right for clearing up outside...

. . . and for collecting pencils.
  'Boris!' said Mrs Prism. 'I don't know how I managed
without you.'

Back at home Maisie was having a lovely time playing school with the kitten when she suddenly looked at her watch.

'Goodness me!' she cried. 'It's time to collect Boris. Someone who hates school won't like to be kept waiting.'

But when Maisie and the kitten arrived, instead of an elephant who hated school, there was a proud, smiling elephant who didn't even notice them at first.

'Well,' said Maisie, 'how do you like school?'
  But Boris wasn't even listening. He was too busy showing the kitten how he could turn into a tree.

Other titles in the Red Fox picture book series (also incorporating Beaver Books)

Not Like That, Like This Tony Bradman & Debbie Van Der Beek
If At First You Do Not See Ruth Brown
I Don't Like It Ruth Brown
The Cross With Us Rhinocerous John Bush & Paul Geraghty
The Proud and Fearless Lion Reg Cartwright
Ellie's Doorstep Alison Catley
Who's Ill Today? Lynne Cherry
Herbie the Dancing Hippo Charlotte Van Emst
The Angel and the Wild Animal Michael Foreman
Joe Eats Bugs Susanne Gretz
Old Bear Jane Hissey
Little Bear's Trousers Jane Hissey
Bad Boris and the birthday Susie Jenkin Pearce
My Grandma Has Black Hair Mary Hoffman and Joanna Burroughs
Best Friends Stephen Kellog
Jake Deborah King
When Sheep Cannot Sleep Satoshi Kitamura
Coco's Birthday Surprise Agnes Matthieu & Angela Sommer-Bodenburg
The Stiltons: Albert and Albertine Moira & Colin Maclean
Not Now, Bernard David McKee
The Sad Story of Veronica who played the Violin David McKee
Snow Woman David McKee
Who's a Clever Baby Then? David McKee
Stories for Summer Alf Prøysen
Mrs Pepperpot and the Macaroni Alf Prøysen
Bad Mood Bear John Richardson
Stone Soup Tony Ross
The Three Pigs Tony Ross
Oscar Got the Blame Tony Ross
A Witch got on at Paddington Station Dyan Sheldon & Wendy Smith
If I were a Crocodile Rowena Sommerville
The Monster Bed Susan Varley & Jeanne Willis
Mucky Mabel Jeanne Willis & Margaret Chamberlain
The Tale of Georgie Grub Jeanne Willis & Margaret Chamberlain
Maggie and the Monster Elizabeth Winthrop & Tomie de Paola